THE MONSTER
MAKER

THE MONSTER MAKER

By Ray Bradbury

Suddenly, it was there. There wasn't time to blink or speak or get scared. Click Hathaway's camera was loaded and he stood there listening to it rack-spin film between his fingers, and he knew he was getting a damned sweet picture of everything that was happening.

The picture of Marnagan hunched huge over the control-console, wrenching levers, jamming studs with freckled fists. And out in the dark of the fore-part there was space and a star-sprinkling and this meteor coming like blazing fury.

Click Hathaway felt the ship move under him like a sensitive animal's skin. And then the meteor hit. It made a spiked fist and knocked the rear-jets flat, and the ship spun like a cosmic merry-go-round.

There was plenty of noise. Too damned much. Hathaway only knew he was picked up and hurled against a lever-bank, and that Marnagan wasn't long in following, swearing loud words. Click remembered hanging on to his camera and gritting to keep holding it. What a sweet shot that had been of the meteor! A sweeter one still of Marnagan beating hell out of the controls and keeping his words to himself until just now.

It got quiet. It got so quiet you could almost hear the asteroids rushing up, cold, blue and hard. You could hear your heart kicking a tom-tom between your sick stomach and your empty lungs.

Stars, asteroids revolved. Click grabbed Marnagan because he was the nearest thing, and held on. You came hunting for a space-raider and you ended up cradled in a slab-sized Irishman's arms, diving at a hunk of metal death. What a fade-out!

"Irish!" he heard himself say. "Is this IT?"

"Is this *what?*" yelled Marnagan inside his helmet.

"Is this where the Big Producer yells CUT!?"

Marnagan fumed. "I'll die when I'm damned good and ready. And when I'm ready I'll inform you and you can picture me profile for Cosmic Films!"

They both waited, thrust against the shipside and held by a hand of gravity; listening to each other's breathing hard in the earphones.

The ship struck, once. Bouncing, it struck again. It turned end over and stopped. Hathaway felt himself grabbed; he and Marnagan rattled around—human dice in a croupier's cup. The shell of the ship burst, air and energy flung out.

Hathaway screamed the air out of his lungs, but his brain was thinking quick crazy, unimportant things. The best scenes in life never reach film, or an audience. Like this one, dammit! Like *this* one! His brain spun, racketing like the instantaneous, flicking motions of his camera.

*

Silence came and engulfed all the noise, ate it up and swallowed it. Hathaway shook his head, instinctively grabbed at the camera locked to his mid-belt. There was nothing but stars, twisted wreckage, cold that pierced through his vac-suit, and silence. He wriggled out of the wreckage into that silence.

He didn't know what he was doing until he found the

camera in his fingers as if it had grown there when he was born. He stood there, thinking "Well, I'll at least have a few good scenes on film. I'll—"

A hunk of metal teetered, fell with a crash. Marnagan elevated seven feet of bellowing manhood from the wreck.

"Hold it!" cracked Hathaway's high voice. Marnagan froze. The camera whirred. "Low angle shot; Interplanetary Patrolman emerges unscathed from asteroid crackup. Swell stuff. I'll get a raise for this!"

"From the toe of me boot!" snarled Marnagan brusquely. Oxen shoulders flexed inside his vac-suit. "I might've died in there, and you nursin' that film-contraption!"

Hathaway felt funny inside, suddenly. "I never thought of that. Marnagan die? I just took it for granted you'd come through. You always have. Funny, but you don't think about dying. You try not to." Hathaway stared at his gloved hand, but the gloving was so thick and heavy he couldn't tell if it was shaking. Muscles in his bony face went down, pale. "Where are we?"

"A million miles from nobody."

They stood in the middle of a pocked, time-eroded meteor plain that stretched off, dipping down into silent indigo and a rash of stars. Overhead, the sun poised; black and stars all around it, making it look sick.

"If we walk in opposite directions, Click Hathaway, we'd be shaking hands the other side of this rock in two hours." Marnagan shook his mop of dusty red hair. "And I promised the boys at Luna Base this time I'd capture that Gunther

THE MONSTER MAKER

lad!"

His voice stopped and the silence spoke.

Hathaway felt his heart pumping slow, hot pumps of blood. "I checked my oxygen, Irish. Sixty minutes of breathing left."

The silence punctuated that sentence, too. Upon the sharp meteoric rocks Hathaway saw the tangled insides of the radio, the food supply mashed and scattered. They were lucky to have escaped. Or *was* suffocation a better death . . . ? *Sixty minutes.*

They stood and looked at one another.

"Damn that meteor!" said Marnagan, hotly.

Hathaway got hold of an idea; remembering something. He said it out: "Somebody tossed that meteor, Irish. I took a picture of it, looked it right in the eye when it rolled at us, and it was poker-hot. Space-meteors are never hot and glowing. If it's proof you want, I've got it here, on film."

Marnagan winced his freckled square of face. "It's not proof we need now, Click. Oxygen. And then *food*. And then some way back to Earth."

Hathaway went on saying his thoughts: "This is Gunther's work. He's here somewhere, probably laughing his guts out at the job he did us. Oh, God, this would make great news-release stuff if we ever get back to Earth. I.P.'s Irish Marnagan, temporarily indisposed by a pirate whose dirty face has never been seen, Gunther by name, finally wins through to a triumphant finish. Photographed on the spot, in color, by yours truly, Click Hathaway. Cosmic Films, please notice."

*

They started walking, fast, over the pocked, rubbled plain toward a bony ridge of metal. They kept their eyes wide and awake. There wasn't much to see, but it was better than standing still, waiting.

Marnagan said, "We're working on margin, and we got nothin' to sweat with except your suspicions about this not being an accident. We got fifty minutes to prove you're right. After that—right or wrong—you'll be Cosmic Films prettiest unmoving, unbreathin' genius. But talk all you like, Click. It's times like this when we all need words, any words, on our tongues. You got your camera and your scoop. Talk about it. As for me—" he twisted his glossy red face. "Keeping alive is me hobby. And this sort of two-bit death I did not order."

Click nodded. "Gunther knows how you'd hate dying this way, Irish. It's irony clean through. That's probably why he planned the meteor and the crash this way."

Marnagan said nothing, but his thick lips went down at the corners, far down, and the green eyes blazed.

They stopped, together.

"Oops!" Click said.

"Hey!" Marnagan blinked. "Did you feel *that?*"

Hathaway's body felt feathery, light as a whisper, boneless and limbless, suddenly. "Irish! We lost weight, coming over that ridge!"

They ran back. "Let's try it again."

They tried it. They scowled at each other. The same thing happened. "Gravity should not act this way, Click."

THE MONSTER MAKER

"Are you telling me? It's man-made. Better than that—it's Gunther! No wonder we fell so fast—we were dragged down by a super-gravity set-up! Gunther'd do anything to—did I say *anything*?"

Hathaway leaped backward in reaction. His eyes widened and his hand came up, jabbing. Over a hill-ridge swarmed a brew of unbelievable horrors. Progeny from Frankenstein's ARK. Immense crimson beasts with numerous legs and gnashing mandibles, brown-black creatures, some tubular and fat, others like thin white poisonous whips slashing along in the air. Fangs caught starlight white on them.

Hathaway yelled and ran, Marnagan at his heels, lumbering. Sweat broke cold on his body. The immense things rolled, slithered and squirmed after him. A blast of light. Marnagan, firing his proton-gun. Then, in Click's ears, the Irishman's incredulous bellow. The gun didn't hurt the creatures at all.

"Irish!" Hathaway flung himself over the ridge, slid down an incline toward the mouth a small cave. "This way, fella!"

Hathaway made it first, Marnagan bellowing just behind him. "They're too big; they can't get us in here!" Click's voice gasped it out, as Marnagan squeezed his two-hundred-fifty pounds beside him. Instinctively, Hathaway added, "Asteroid monsters! My camera! What a scene!"

"Damn your damn camera!" yelled Marnagan. "They might come in!"

"Use your gun."

"They got impervious hides. No use. Gahh! And that was a pretty chase, eh, Click?"

"Yeah. Sure. *You* enjoyed it, every moment of it."

"I did that." Irish grinned, showing white uneven teeth. "Now, what will we be doing with these uninvited guests at our door?"

"Let me think—"

"Lots of time, little man. Forty more minutes of air, to be exact."

*

They sat, staring at the monsters for about a minute. Hathaway felt funny about something; didn't know what. Something about these monsters and Gunther and—

"Which one will you be having?" asked Irish, casually. "A red one or a blue one?"

Hathaway laughed nervously. "A pink one with yellow ruffles—Good God, now you've got *me* doing it. Joking in the face of death."

"Me father taught me; keep laughing and you'll have Irish luck."

That didn't please the photographer. "I'm an Anglo-Swede," he pointed out.

Marnagan shifted uneasily. "Here, now. You're doing nothing but sitting, looking like a little boy locked in a bedroom closet, so take me a profile shot of the beasties and myself."

Hathaway petted his camera reluctantly. "What in hell's the use? All this swell film shot. Nobody'll ever see it."

"Then," retorted Marnagan, "we'll develop it for our own benefit; while waitin' for the U.S. Cavalry to come riding over

11

the hill to our rescue!"

Hathaway snorted. "U.S. Cavalry."

Marnagan raised his proton-gun dramatically. "Snap me this pose," he said. "I paid your salary to trot along, photographing, we hoped, my capture of Gunther, now the least you can do is record peace negotiations betwixt me and these pixies."

Marnagan wasn't fooling anybody. Hathaway knew the superficial palaver for nothing but a covering over the fast, furious thinking running around in that red-cropped skull. Hathaway played the palaver, too, but his mind was whirring faster than his camera as he spun a picture of Marnagan standing there with a useless gun pointed at the animals.

Montage. Marnagan sitting, chatting at the monsters. Marnagan smiling for the camera. Marnagan in profile. Marnagan looking grim, without much effort, for the camera. And then, a closeup of the thrashing death wall that holed them in. Click took them all, those shots, not saying anything. Nobody fooled nobody with this act. Death was near and they had sweaty faces, dry mouths and frozen guts.

When Click finished filming, Irish sat down to save oxygen, and used it up arguing about Gunther. Click came back at him:

"Gunther drew us down here, sure as Ceres! That gravity change we felt back on that ridge, Irish; that proves it. Gunther's short on men. So, what's he do; he builds an asteroid-base, and drags ships down. Space war isn't perfect yet, guns don't prime true in space, trajectory is lousy over long distances. So what's the best weapon, which dispenses with losing valuable, rare ships and a small bunch of men? Super-gravity and a couple of well-tossed meteors. Saves all around. It's a good front, this damned iron pebble. From it, Gunther strikes unseen; ships simply crash, that's all. A subtle hand, with all aces."

Marnagan rumbled. "Where is the dirty son, then!"

"He didn't have to appear, Irish. He sent—them." Hathaway nodded at the beasts. "People crashing here die from air-lack, no food, or from wounds caused at the crackup. If they survive all that—the animals tend to them. It all looks like Nature was responsible. See how subtle his attack is? Looks like accidental death instead of murder, if the Patrol happens to land and finds us. No reason for undue investigation, then."

"I don't see no Base around."

*

Click shrugged. "Still doubt it? Okay. Look." He tapped his camera and a spool popped out onto his gloved palm. Holding it up, he stripped it out to its full twenty inch length, held it to the light while it developed, smiling. It was one of his best inventions. Self-developing film. The first light struck film-surface, destroyed one chemical, leaving imprints; the second exposure simply hardened, secured the impressions. Quick stuff.

Inserting the film-tongue into a micro-viewer in the camera's base, Click handed the whole thing over. "Look."

Marnagan put the viewer up against the helmet glass,

13

squinted. "Ah, Click. Now, now. This is one lousy film you invented."

"Huh?"

"It's a strange process'll develop my picture and ignore the asteroid monsters complete."

"What!"

Hathaway grabbed the camera, gasped, squinted, and gasped again: Pictures in montage; Marnagan sitting down, chatting conversationally with *nothing*; Marnagan shooting his gun at *nothing*; Marnagan pretending to be happy in front of *nothing*.

Then, closeup—of—NOTHING!

The monsters had failed to image the film. Marnagan was there, his hair like a red banner, his freckled face with the blue eyes bright in it. Maybe—

Hathaway said it, loud: "Irish! Irish! I think I see a way out of this mess! Here—"

He elucidated it over and over again to the Patrolman. About the film, the beasts, and how the film couldn't be wrong. If the film said the monsters weren't there, they weren't there.

"Yeah," said Marnagan. "But step outside this cave—"

"If my theory is correct I'll do it, unafraid," said Click.

Marnagan scowled. "You sure them beasts don't radiate ultra-violet or infra-red or something that won't come out on film?"

"Nuts! Any color *we* see, the camera sees. We've been

fooled."

"Hey, where *you* going?" Marnagan blocked Hathaway as the smaller man tried pushing past him.

"Get out of the way," said Hathaway.

Marnagan put his big fists on his hips. "If anyone is going anywhere, it'll be me does the going."

"I can't let you do that, Irish."

"Why not?"

"You'd be going on my say-so."

"Ain't your say-so good enough for me?"

"Yes. Sure. Of course. I guess—"

"If you say them animals ain't there, that's all I need. Now, stand aside, you film-developing flea, and let an Irishman settle their bones." He took an unnecessary hitch in trousers that didn't exist except under an inch of porous metal plate. "Your express purpose on this voyage, Hathaway, is taking films to be used by the Patrol later for teaching Junior Patrolmen how to act in tough spots. First-hand education. Poke another spool of film in that contraption and give me profile a scan. This is lesson number seven: Daniel Walks Into The Lion's Den."

"Irish, I—"

"Shut up and load up."

Hathaway nervously loaded the film-slot, raised it.

"Ready, Click?"

"I—I guess so," said Hathaway. "And remember, think it hard, Irish. Think it hard. There aren't any animals—"

"Keep me in focus, lad."

THE MONSTER MAKER

"All the way, Irish."

"What do they say . . . ? Oh, yeah. Action. Lights. Camera!"

Marnagan held his gun out in front of him and still smiling took one, two, three, four steps out into the outside world. The monsters were waiting for him at the fifth step. Marnagan kept walking.

Right out into the middle of them . . . .

*

That was the sweetest shot Hathaway ever took. Marnagan and the monsters!

Only now it was only Marnagan.

No more monsters.

Marnagan smiled a smile broader than his shoulders. "Hey, Click, look at me! I'm in one piece. Why, hell, the damned things turned tail and ran away!"

"Ran, hell!" cried Hathaway, rushing out, his face flushed and animated. "They just plain vanished. They were only imaginative figments!"

"And to think we let them hole us in that way, Click Hathaway, you coward!"

"Smile when you say that, Irish."

"Sure, and ain't I always smilin'? Ah, Click boy, are them tears in your sweet grey eyes?"

"Damn," swore the photographer, embarrassedly. "Why don't they put window-wipers in these helmets?"

"I'll take it up with the Board, lad."

"Forget it. I was so blamed glad to see your homely carcass in one hunk, I couldn't help—Look, now, about Gunther.

Those animals are part of his set-up. Explorers who land here inadvertently, are chased back into their ships, forced to take off. Tourists and the like. Nothing suspicious about animals. And if the tourists don't leave, the animals kill them."

"Shaw, now. Those animals can't kill."

"Think not, Mr. Marnagan? As long as we believed in them they could have frightened us to death, forced us, maybe, to commit suicide. If that isn't being dangerous—"

The Irishman whistled.

"But, we've got to *move*, Irish. We've got twenty minutes of oxygen. In that time we've got to trace those monsters to their source, Gunther's Base, fight our way in, and get fresh oxy-cannisters." Click attached his camera to his mid-belt. "Gunther probably thinks we're dead by now. Everyone else's been fooled by his playmates; they never had a chance to disbelieve them."

"If it hadn't been for you taking them pictures, Click—"

"Coupled with your damned stubborn attitude about the accident—" Click stopped and felt his insides turning to water. He shook his head and felt a film slip down over his eyes. He spread his legs out to steady himself, and swayed. "I—I don't think my oxygen is as full as yours. This excitement had me double-breathing and I feel sick."

Marnagan's homely face grimaced in sympathy. "Hold tight, Click. The guy that invented these fish-bowls didn't provide for a sick stomach."

"Hold tight, hell, let's move. We've got to find where those animals came from! And the only way to do that is to get the animals to come back!"

"Come back? How?"

"They're waiting, just outside the aura of our thoughts, and if we believe in them again, they'll return."

Marnagan didn't like it. "Won't—won't they kill us—if they come—if we believe in 'em?"

Hathaway shook a head that was tons heavy and weary. "Not if we believe in them to a *certain point*. Psychologically they can both be seen and felt. We only want to *see* them coming at us again."

"*Do* we, now?"

"With twenty minutes left, maybe less—"

"All right, Click, let's bring 'em back. How do we do it?"

Hathaway fought against the mist in his eyes. "Just think—I will see the monsters again. I will see them again and I will not feel them. Think it over and over."

Marnagan's hulk stirred uneasily. "And—what if I forget to remember all that? What if I get excited . . . ?"

Hathaway didn't answer. But his eyes told the story by just looking at Irish.

Marnagan cursed. "All right, lad. Let's have at it!"

The monsters returned.

*

A soundless deluge of them, pouring over the rubbled horizon, swarming in malevolent anticipation about the two men.

"This way, Irish. They come from this way! There's a focal point, a sending station for these telepathic brutes. Come on!"

Hathaway sludged into the pressing tide of color, mouths, contorted faces, silvery fat bodies misting as he plowed through them.

Marnagan was making good progress ahead of Hathaway. But he stopped and raised his gun and made quick moves with it. "Click! This one here! It's real!" He fell back and something struck him down. His immense frame slammed against rock, noiselessly.

Hathaway darted forward, flung his body over Marnagan's, covered the helmet glass with his hands, shouting:

"Marnagan! Get a grip, dammit! It's not real—don't let it force into your mind! It's not real, I tell you!"

"Click—" Marnagan's face was a bitter, tortured movement behind glass. "Click—" He was fighting hard. "I—I—sure now. Sure—" He smiled. "It—it's only a shanty fake!"

"Keep saying it, Irish. Keep it up."

Marnagan's thick lips opened. "It's only a fake," he said. And then, irritated, "Get the hell off me, Hathaway. Let me up to my feet!"

Hathaway got up, shakily. The air in his helmet smelled stale, and little bubbles danced in his eyes. "Irish, you forget the monsters. Let me handle them, I know how. They might fool you again, you might forget."

Marnagan showed his teeth. "Gah! Let a flea have all the fun? And besides, Click, I like to look at them. They're pretty."

The outpour of animals came from a low lying mound a

mile farther on. Evidently the telepathic source lay there. They approached it warily.

"We'll be taking our chances on guard," hissed Irish. "I'll go ahead, draw their attention, maybe get captured. Then, *you* show up with *your* gun . . . . "

"I haven't got one."

"We'll chance it, then. You stick here until I see what's ahead. They probably got scanners out. Let them see me—"

And before Hathaway could object, Marnagan walked off. He walked about five hundred yards, bent down, applied his fingers to something, heaved up, and there was a door opening in the rock.

His voice came back across the distance, into Click's earphones. "A door, an air-lock, Click. A tunnel leading down inside!"

Then, Marnagan dropped into the tunnel, disappearing. Click heard the thud of his feet hitting the metal flooring.

Click sucked in his breath, hard and fast.

"All right, put 'em up!" a new harsh voice cried over a different radio. One of Gunther's guards.

Three shots sizzled out, and Marnagan bellowed.

The strange harsh voice said, "That's better. Don't try and pick that gun up now. Oh, so it's you. I thought Gunther had finished you off. How'd you get past the animals?"

Click started running. He switched off his *sending* audio, kept his *receiving* on. Marnagan, weaponless. *One* guard. Click gasped. Things were getting dark. Had to have air. Air. Air. He ran and kept running and listening to Marnagan's lying voice:

"I tied them pink elephants of Gunther's in neat alphabetical bundles and stacked them up to dry, ya louse!" Marnagan said. "But, damn you, they killed my partner before he had a chance!"

The guard laughed.

*

The air-lock door was still wide open when Click reached it, his head swimming darkly, his lungs crammed with pain-fire and hell-rockets. He let himself down in, quiet and soft. He didn't have a weapon. He didn't have a weapon. Oh, damn, damn!

A tunnel curved, ending in light, and two men silhouetted in that yellow glare. Marnagan, backed against a wall, his helmet cracked, air hissing slowly out of it, his face turning blue. And the guard, a proton gun extended stiffly before him, also in a vac-suit. The guard had his profile toward Hathaway, his lips twisting: "I think I'll let you stand right there and die," he said quietly. "That what Gunther wanted, anway. A nice sordid death."

Hathaway took three strides, his hands out in front of him.

"Don't move!" he snapped. "I've got a weapon stronger than yours. One twitch and I'll blast you and the whole damned wall out from behind you! Freeze!"

The guard whirled. He widened his sharp eyes, and reluctantly, dropped his gun to the floor.

"Get his gun, Irish."

Marnagan made as if to move, crumpled clumsily forward.

THE MONSTER MAKER

Hathaway ran in, snatched up the gun, smirked at the guard. "Thanks for posing," he said. "That shot will go down in film history for candid acting."

"What!"

"Ah: ah! Keep your place. I've got a real gun now. Where's the door leading into the Base?"

The guard moved his head sullenly over his left shoulder.

Click was afraid he would show his weak dizziness. He needed air. "Okay. Drag Marnagan with you, open the door and we'll have air. Double time! Double!"

Ten minutes later, Marnagan and Hathaway, fresh tanks of oxygen on their backs, Marnagan in a fresh bulger and helmet, trussed the guard, hid him in a huge trash receptacle. "Where he belongs," observed Irish tersely.

They found themselves in a complete inner world; an asteroid nothing more than a honey-comb fortress sliding through the void unchallenged. Perfect front for a raider who had little equipment and was short-handed of men. Gunther simply waited for specific cargo ships to rocket by, pulled them or knocked them down and swarmed over them for cargo. The animals served simply to insure against suspicion and the swarms of tourists that filled the void these days. Small fry weren't wanted. They were scared off.

The telepathic sending station for the animals was a great bank of intricate, glittering machine, through which strips of colored film with images slid into slots and machine mouths that translated them into thought-emanations. A damned neat piece of genius.

"So here we are, still not much better off than we were," growled Irish. "We haven't a ship or a space-radio, and more guards'll turn up any moment. You think we could refocus this doohingey, project the monsters inside the asteroid to fool the pirates themselves?"

"What good would that do?" Hathaway gnawed his lip. "They wouldn't fool the engineers who created them, you nut."

Marnagan exhaled disgustedly. "Ah, if only the U.S. Cavalry would come riding over the hill—"

*

"Irish!" Hathaway snapped that, his face lighting up. "Irish. The U.S. Cavalry it is!" His eyes darted over the machines. "Here. Help me. We'll stage everything on the most colossal raid of the century."

Marnagan winced. "You breathing oxygen or whiskey?"

"There's only one stipulation I make, Irish. I want a complete picture of Marnagan capturing Raider's Base. I want a picture of Gunther's face when you do it. Snap it, now, we've got rush work to do. How good an actor are you?"

"That's a silly question."

"You only have to do three things. Walk with your gun out in front of you, firing. That's number one. Number two is to clutch at your heart and fall down dead. Number three is to clutch at your side, fall down and twitch on the ground. Is that clear?"

"Clear as the Coal Sack Nebula . . . . "

An hour later Hathaway trudged down a passageway that

led out into a sort of city street inside the asteroid. There were about six streets, lined with cube houses in yellow metal, ending near Hathaway in a wide, green-lawned Plaza.

Hathaway, weaponless, idly carrying his camera in one hand, walked across the Plaza as if he owned it. He was heading for a building that was pretentious enough to be Gunther's quarters.

He got halfway there when he felt a gun in his back.

He didn't resist. They took him straight ahead to his destination and pushed him into a room where Gunther sat.

Hathaway looked at him. "So you're Gunther?" he said, calmly. The pirate was incredibly old, his bulging forehead stood out over sunken, questioningly dark eyes, and his scrawny body was lost in folds of metal-link cloth. He glanced up from a paper-file, surprised. Before he could speak, Hathaway said:

"Everything's over with, Mr. Gunther. The Patrol is in the city now and we're capturing your Base. Don't try to fight. We've a thousand men against your eighty-five."

Gunther sat there, blinking at Hathaway, not moving. His thin hands twitched in his lap. "You are bluffing," he said, finally, with a firm directness. "A ship hasn't landed here for an hour. Your ship was the last. Two people were on it. The last I saw of them they were being pursued to the death by the Beasts. One of you escaped, it seemed."

"Both. The other guy went after the Patrol."

"Impossible!"

"I can't respect your opinion, Mr. Gunther."

A shouting rose from the Plaza. About fifty of Gunther's men, lounging on carved benches during their time-off, stirred to their feet and started yelling. Gunther turned slowly to the huge window in one side of his office. He stared, hard.

The Patrol was coming!

Across the Plaza, marching quietly and decisively, came the Patrol. Five hundred Patrolmen in one long, incredible line, carrying paralysis guns with them in their tight hands.

Gunther babbled like a child, his voice a shrill dagger in the air. "Get out there, you men! Throw them back! We're outnumbered!"

Guns flared. But the Patrol came on. Gunther's men didn't run, Hathaway had to credit them on that. They took it, standing.

Hathaway chuckled inside, deep. What a sweet, sweet shot this was. His camera whirred, clicked and whirred again. Nobody stopped him from filming it. Everything was too wild, hot and angry. Gunther was throwing a fit, still seated at his desk, unable to move because of his fragile, bony legs and their atrophied state.

Some of the Patrol were killed. Hathaway chuckled again as he saw three of the Patrolmen clutch at their hearts, crumple, lie on the ground and twitch. God, what photography!

Gunther raged, and swept a small pistol from his linked corselet. He fired wildly until Hathaway hit him over the head with a paper-weight. Then Hathaway took a picture of Gunther slumped at his desk, the chaos taking place immediately outside his window.

THE MONSTER MAKER

The pirates broke and fled, those that were left. A mere handful. And out of the chaos came Marnagan's voice, "Here!"

*

One of the Patrolmen stopped firing, and ran toward Click and the Building. He got inside. "Did you see them run, Click boy? What an idea. How did we do?"

"Fine, Irish. Fine!"

"So here's Gunther, the spalpeen! Gunther, the little dried up pirate, eh?" Marnagan whacked Hathaway on the back. "I'll have to hand it to you, this is the best plan o' battle ever laid out. And proud I was to fight with such splendid men as these—" He gestured toward the Plaza.

Click laughed with him. "You should be proud. Five hundred Patrolmen with hair like red banners flying, with thick Irish brogues and broad shoulders and freckles and blue eyes and a body as tall as your stories!"

Marnagan roared. "I always said, I said—if ever there could be an army of Marnagans, we could lick the whole damn uneeverse! Did you photograph it, Click?"

"I did." Hathaway tapped his camera happily.

"Ah, then, won't that be a scoop for you, boy? Money from the Patrol so they can use the film as instruction in Classes and money from Cosmic Films for the news-reel headlines! And what a scene, and what acting! Five hundred duplicates of Steve Marnagan, broadcast telepathically into the minds of the pirates, walking across a Plaza, capturing the whole she-bang! How did you like my death-scenes?"

"You're a ham. And anyway—five hundred duplicates, nothing!" said Click. He ripped the film-spool from the camera, spread it in the air to develop, inserted it in the micro-viewer. "Have a look—"

Marnagan looked. "Ah, now. Ah, now," he said over and over. "There's the Plaza, and there's Gunther's men fighting and then they're turning and running. And what are they running from? One man! Me. Irish Marnagan! Walking all by myself across the lawn, paralyzing them. One against a hundred, and the cowards running from me!

"Sure, Click, this is better than I thought. I forgot that the film wouldn't register telepathic emanations, them other Marnagans. It makes it look like I'm a mighty brave man, does it not? It does. Ah, look—look at me, Hathaway, I'm enjoying every minute of it, I am."

*

Hathaway swatted him on his back-side. "Look here, you egocentric son of Erin, there's more work to be done. More pirates to be captured. The Patrol is still marching around and someone might be suspicious if they looked too close and saw all that red hair."

"All right, Click, we'll clean up the rest of them now. We're a combination, we two, we are. I take it all back about your pictures, Click, if you hadn't thought of taking pictures of me and inserting it into those telepath machines we'd be dead ducks now. Well—here I go . . . . "

Hathaway stopped him. "Hold it. Until I load my camera again."

Irish grinned. "Hurry it up. Here come three guards. They're unarmed. I think I'll handle them with me fists for a change. The gentle art of uppercuts. Are you ready, Hathaway?"

"Ready."

Marnagan lifted his big ham-fists.

The camera whirred. Hathaway chuckled, to himself.

What a sweet fade-out this was!

www.ingramcontent.com/pod-product-compliance
Lightning Source LLC
Chambersburg PA
CBHW050910120626
46554CB00003B/1111